GREAT DINOSAUR HUNTERS

For a free color catalog describing Gareth Stevens' list of high-quality books and multimedia programs, call 1-800-542-2595 (USA) or 1-800-461-9120 (Canada). Gareth Stevens Publishing's Fax: (414) 225-0377.

Library of Congress Cataloging-in-Publication Data

Green, Tamara, 1945-
    Great dinosaur hunters/by Tamara Green; illustrated by Richard Grant.
        p. cm. — (World of dinosaurs)
    Includes bibliographical references and index.
    Summary: Recounts how different professional and amateur fossil-hunters
discovered the remains of many different species of dinosaurs.
    ISBN 0-8368-2291-9 (lib. bdg.)
    1. Paleontologists—Juvenile literature. 2. Paleontology—Juvenile
literature. 3. Dinosaurs—Juvenile literature. [1. Paleontology.
2. Paleontologists. 3. Fossils. 4. Dinosaurs.] I. Grant, Richard, 1959- ill.
II. Title. III. Series: World of dinosaurs.
QE707.A2G74   1999
560'.92'2—dc21   98-31768

This North American edition first published in 1999 by
Gareth Stevens Publishing
1555 North RiverCenter Drive, Suite 201
Milwaukee, Wisconsin 53212 USA

This U.S. edition © 1999 by Gareth Stevens, Inc.
Created with original © 1998 by Quartz Editorial Services,
112 Station Road, Edgware HA8 7AQ U.K.
Additional end matter © 1999 by Gareth Stevens, Inc.

Consultant: Dr. Paul Barrett, Paleontologist, Specialist in Biology and
  Evolution of Dinosaurs, University of Cambridge, England.

Printed in Mexico

1 2 3 4 5 6 7 8 9 03 02 01 00 99

GREAT DINOSAUR HUNTERS

by Tamara Green
Illustrated by Richard Grant

Gareth Stevens Publishing
MILWAUKEE

CONTENTS

INTRODUCTION

It is not hard to imagine the excitement when, after days of backbreaking digging, a dinosaur skeleton is finally unearthed — after having been buried for 150 million years or more. It may be more difficult to imagine, however, the brawls that broke out in parts of western North America during the late nineteenth century over these fossilized remains and who had found them first.

Perhaps it is not all that surprising; after all, there were rich rewards for those hunters who were successful in exposing the bones of such marvelous creatures as **Diplodocus** and **Stegosaurus**.

Recently, well over 100 years after these earlier dinosaur disputes, landowners and dinosaur hunters engaged in legal battles in court over the remains of a **Tyrannosaurus rex**, nicknamed Sue. Fortunately, the matter has been resolved, and the skeleton is now held by the Field Museum of Natural History in Chicago, Illinois.

It is not only professional paleontologists who have become famous for their discoveries in the field. Many fantastic and important finds have been made by amateur fossil-hunters and dinosaur enthusiasts.

We invite you now to meet many of the world's most successful dinosaur hunters, some of whom have had dinosaurs named after them. New dinosaur finds are being made all the time, all around the world; if you should ever discover the remains of a dinosaur, maybe they will name it after *you*!

DINOSAUR NAMES

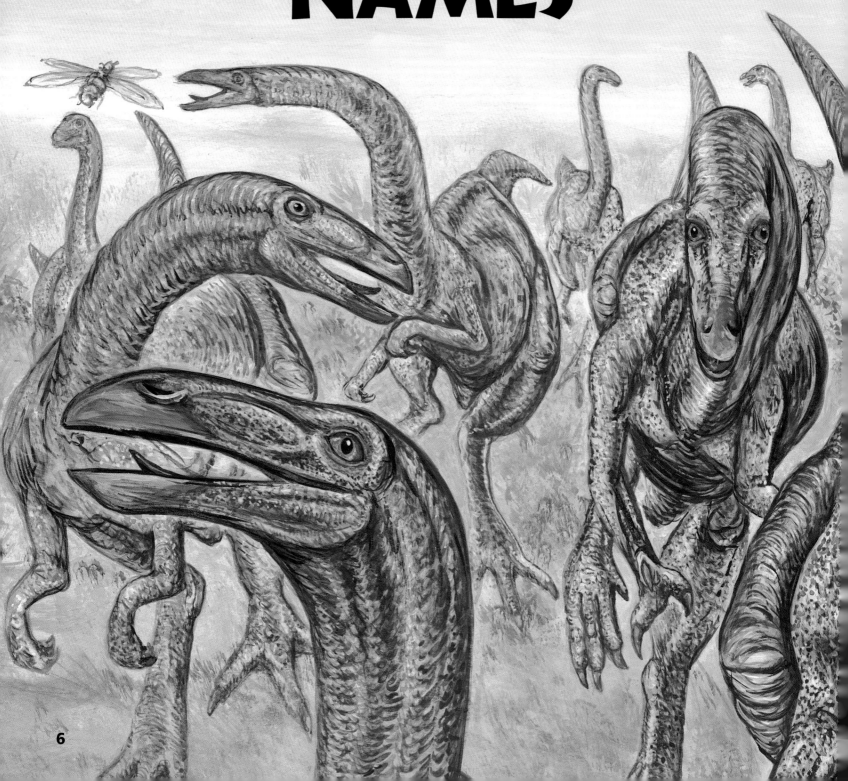

When new dinosaurs are discovered, they have to be named. How are these names chosen, and by whom?

The herd of **Ornithomimus** started to run, aware of the sudden approach of a hungry carnivore. They had a very distinctive, almost ostrichlike appearance and were fleet of foot, so there was a good chance they would be able to escape.

Like **Ornithomimus**, whose name means "bird mimic," many dinosaurs have been given names that relate to some aspect of their appearance or behavior. For example, **Maiasaura**, a Cretaceous plant-eater from North America, has a name meaning "good mother lizard." Its remains were found close to its nest, with the skeletons of several of its young nearby. (Find out more about its discovery and paleontologist Jack Horner on page 27.)

In other cases, dinosaurs have been named after the area where their remains were unearthed. The Jurassic sauropod **Patagosaurus**, for example, is named after Patagonia, in Argentina, South America. **Camelotia**, a Late Triassic prosauropod, is named after the site of King Arthur's legendary court, Camelot, supposedly in southwest England where this dinosaur was dug up.

Sometimes dinosaurs are named after people. The Late Cretaceous plant-eater **Parkosaurus**, found in Canada, was named in honor of William A. Parks, an authority on dinosaurs from that part of the world. Another herbivore, the dinosaur **Leaellynosaurus**, was named after the young daughter of the two Australian paleontologists who first unearthed it. Its name means "Leaellyn's lizard."

RICHARD 'OLD BONES' OWEN

British scientist Sir Richard Owen (1804-1892), nicknamed "Old Bones" because of his interest in anatomy, first coined the word *dinosaur*. The term is derived from two Greek words — *deinos*, meaning "fearfully big" and *sauros*, meaning "a lizard." We now know, of course, that not all dinosaurs were huge. Owen, however, was convinced that dinosaurs were different from any other creatures known, and merited having a name of their own.

DINO WARS

Just as dinosaurs fought in prehistoric times, millions of years later American paleontologists engaged in combat over who had found which skeletal remains first — and who could claim them.

The roar of the **Daspletosaurus** echoed over the Cretaceous landscape of a region that is now in North America. It opened its massive jaws and prepared to pounce on its next meal. **Daspletosaurus** was a member of the same group of dinosaurs to which **Tyrannosaurus rex** belonged; though not as large, it was forever on the prowl. Its prey did not dare look back, aware that every second counted when a 28-foot (8.5-meter)-long flesh-eater with daggerlike fangs was in hot pursuit.

The race was on — just as it was to be some 90 million years later, as two gifted paleontologists from North America battled over dinosaur finds in the same region. Both Othniel Marsh and Edward Drinker Cope had his own team of collectors. As they unearthed fossils at the excavation site, they would send the specimens back to headquarters for identification and further study. So it was that the very first bones found from a **Stegosaurus** skeleton were sent by rail to Marsh in 1877, the same year that those of a sauropod to be named **Camarasaurus** were delivered to Cope for study and identification.

Competition between the two scientists was fierce. It is even rumored that on one occasion a prospector for Cope pretended to be a traveler selling groceries, while he secretly spied on what the rivals had unearthed that day.

This was war, even if on a small scale. Sometimes the teams would threaten each other, or would even engage in fistfights over particular bones. There were times, too, when men would desert one team and join the other, probably as a result of bribes. Bones were sometimes broken and destroyed if they could not be dug up immediately, simply so that the other party would not find them and

benefit. It may be hard to believe that two such respected and knowledgeable men could have headed teams that resorted to behavior of this kind, but

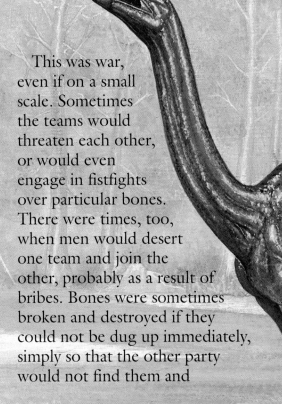

their interest in fossils had become obsessive. Many of their finds are on display today in natural history museums in the United States.

TWO GREAT RIVALS

E. D. Cope, *right*, and O. C. Marsh, *below*, were bitter nineteenth-century rivals. They went out of their way to keep the sites of their proposed dinosaur digs secret and even set false trails to deter the other team from getting there first.

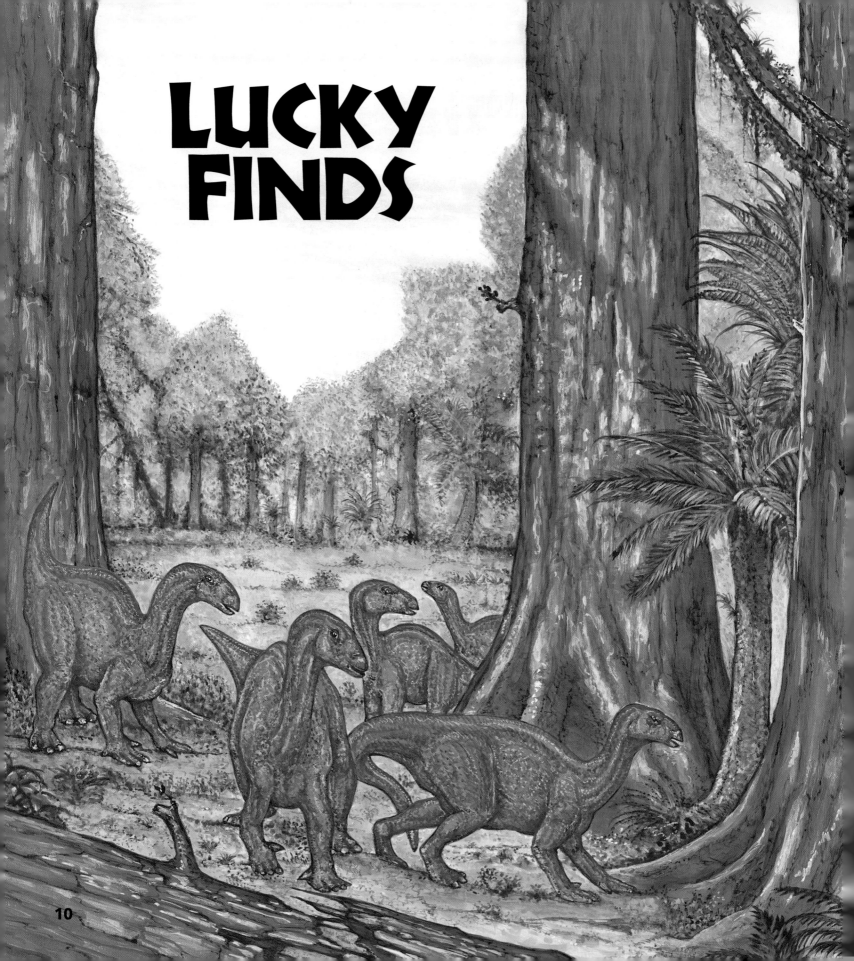

LUCKY FINDS

Sometimes, important remains from new species of dinosaurs are discovered accidentally.

A lively group of very young **Iguanodon** scampered beneath the huge trees. It would be years before they were long and strong enough to balance on their hind legs and reach up to browse on the foliage of giant oaks. Until then, these juvenile Cretaceous herbivores would feed by snapping off low-growing plants with their toothless beaks. They would then chomp on the crisp vegetation, using rows of tough cheek teeth.

Seventy million years later, one of these **Iguanodon** teeth was discovered by Mary Mantell, *bottom right*, in Sussex, England. It was the first of many fossil finds made of this species of dinosaur.

Often, a team of paleontologists sets out on a dig because the group has a good reason to be looking for remains in a particular region. Fossils may have been dug up or discovered nearby on some previous occasion. Occasionally, however, a major fossil discovery comes as a complete surprise.

Take, for instance, the unearthing of **Muttaburrasaurus**, believed by some experts to have been a plant-eater and by others to have been an omnivore. This Cretaceous dinosaur resembled **Iguanodon** in many respects, having a similar thumb weapon for use in self-defense.

Curious cattle

In 1963, an Australian cattle rancher noticed something unusual. Some of the animals in the herd were sniffing around by the banks of the Thomson River in Queensland. They had scattered some bones in their activity, so the rancher, named Langdon, went over to investigate. He was startled to find that his cattle had disturbed what appeared to him to be the remains of a dinosaur.

When paleontologists from the Queensland Museum came to investigate the site, Langdon's suspicions were confirmed. In fact, a new species of dinosaur had been unearthed! Scientists named this new dinosaur **Muttaburrasaurus langdoni**, after the rancher who first reported his cattle's chance discovery.

If you ever find what you think might be dinosaur bones, or the remains of some other prehistoric creature, paleontologists recommend that you do not remove what you have found. Instead, it is best to immediately contact a natural history museum, so that experts can be sure no damage is done in unearthing what could be very valuable remains — perhaps of an entirely new dinosaur species.

MARY MANTELL

Mary Ann Mantell, wife of the nineteenth-century British doctor and scientist Gideon Mantell, was strolling in Sussex, England, when she suddenly caught sight of a tooth embedded in rock. Mary took it to her husband, who described it as a "large tooth which, from the worn, smooth, and oblique surface of the crown had evidently belonged to an herbivorous animal." The rock had originally been removed from a local quarry, and a number of bones were found there, too — all later identified as **Iguanodon** remains, thanks to Mary's discovery and action.

AFRICAN DISCOVERY

When an engineer prospecting for minerals came across a few fossils in what was then German East Africa, he could not have imagined what would be unearthed as a result over the next few years.

A tremendously tall and bulky **Brachiosaurus** surveyed the Jurassic landscape of what is now Tanzania, Africa, pausing for a while before it began to feed again from the treetops. Human beings had not yet evolved, of course. Some 170 million years later, however, they were to discover this dinosaur's fossilized remains in an open-cast quarry in a region that became known as Tendaguru.

A mineral prospector first discovered giant fossils in Tanzania in 1907. Not long afterward, a German museum raised funds so that a major four-year expedition could be undertaken to that region of Africa. This project, led by Dr. Werner Janensch, was the biggest of its kind to date and involved several hundred local men and their families.

WERNER JANENSCH

The German museum curator who led expeditions to Africa during which important remains of **Brachiosaurus** were found is shown *below*. Janensch and some of his many assistants are seen posing with one of the giant sauropod's bones. He was also assisted by Edwin Hennig from the Berlin Museum of Natural History.

Bone bonanza

The area to be excavated covered about 5 miles (8 kilometers). During the expedition, thousands of bones were unearthed — some from carnivores, some from herbivores. After removal, these fossils had to be wrapped for protection, then transported individually by hand to the nearest port. This tedious and painstaking procedure

involved countless treks of up to four days each. In some instances, a whole team of local men would be assigned to carry a single vertebra, because the bones were so huge and heavy. In all, 250 tons of fossils were shipped to the museum in Berlin, Germany, where the task of cleaning and classifying could at last begin. This process, too, took many years of effort; the finds were finally placed on public view in 1920, over ten years after they had been found. The unearthing of an almost complete **Brachiosaurus** was a major feat. Its reconstruction is the largest mounted skeleton in the world — standing at 40 feet (12 m) tall and over 74 feet (22 m) in length. It can be seen in the Museum of Natural History of Humbolt University, in Berlin, Germany.

FOSSIL-HUNTER WITH FLAIR

14

Mary Anning's fossil shop in Lyme Regis, England, must have been a wonderful place for adults and children to explore!

The two children were so excited they could hardly contain their enthusiasm. They knew, however, that nineteenth-century British society required that they remain well-mannered and quiet until they were back in the privacy of their own home.

On the south coast of England, in the seaside town of Lyme Regis, stood a tiny, rather dingy shop that they loved to visit whenever they had a chance — it contained the most amazing selection of fossils and shells imaginable.

A few pennies went a long way in 1827 and would buy them a whole bag of treasures. What was more, their father had built a cabinet so that they could display their growing collection. Soon it would be filled to capacity.

What the children found most fascinating of all during their visits to this little shop was that the proprietor — a woman named Mary Anning — would spend time guiding them as to what they might buy. She could tell them precisely how and where she had found these items, and what the creatures were like when alive.

In fact, Mary Anning would go down to the pebbly beach at Lyme Regis every day to search for fossilized remains under the hanging cliffs, before there was any risk they might be washed away by the ocean's tides. Some of her finds would serve to restock the shop's substantial inventory; others proved so valuable and unique that they merited serious scientific study.

> *Miss Anning, as a child, ne'er passed*
> *A pin upon the ground;*
> *But picked it up, and so at last*
> *An ichthyosaurus found.*

Mary was the second child of Richard and Milly Anning. Her father had instilled in her an interest in fossils, since he collected and sold them to supplement his income. Even when quite young, Mary and her brother would join their father fossil-hunting on the beach, where they both learned about paleontology at his side.

When Mary's father died, the family found themselves struggling financially. They decided to continue collecting and marketing fossils, which proved to be a very wise decision. The Annings soon became well-known locally for their discoveries, as well as for their interesting shop. As things turned out, the family did quite well because some of Mary's rarest finds brought in significant income.

One of Mary's greatest skills was her natural ability to put together fossilized remains. She could reconstruct, or rebuild, the original skeleton of a prehistoric creature with astounding accuracy, even though she had no academic training in this science. She was also the first person to unearth a complete plesiosaur skeleton. Her other finds included pterosaur and ichthyosaur skeletons.

It was highly unusual at the time for a woman to be so involved in this type of work, yet many of the most highly renowned collectors and geologists greatly respected her contribution to their science. In fact, when she became ill toward the end of her life, various academic bodies made sure that she had enough money to support her modest lifestyle. Later, a road in the town of Lyme Regis, England, was named after her. She was also honored by the rhyme *at left*, which was composed in 1884.

DISCOVERY

William Buckland

William Buckland (1784-1856) was the first to describe the skeleton of a **Megalosaurus**. He thought the heavily built carnivore, which was 30 feet (9 m) long, was a giant lizard.

William Walker

The highly talented British amateur fossil-hunter William Walker first discovered a claw of the Early Cretaceous fish-eating dinosaur **Baryonyx** in 1983.

Tyrannosaurus rex

Natural history museums in Pittsburgh, Pennsylvania, and New York City, New York, house remains of Cretaceous **Tyrannosaurus rex**, which were found by the great American dinosaur-hunter Barnum Brown (1873-1963) in Montana.

GALLERY-1

Seismosaurus

With a name meaning "earth-shaking lizard," Late Jurassic **Seismosaurus**, found in New Mexico, is reputedly the world's longest dinosaur at a staggering 108 feet (33 m). It was excavated by American paleontologist David Gillette in 1985.

Carnotaurus

In 1985, the leading Argentinian dinosaurologist, José F. Bonaparte, named this Early Cretaceous predator **Carnotaurus**. The strange meat-eater was 25 feet (7.6 m) long and had a bull-like head and rough skin, as shown *at right*.

Muttaburrasaurus

Ralph E. Molnar, an American working in Australia in 1981, described this remarkable 23-foot (7-m)-long Cretaceous find, **Muttaburrasaurus**, with its characteristic thumb spikes.

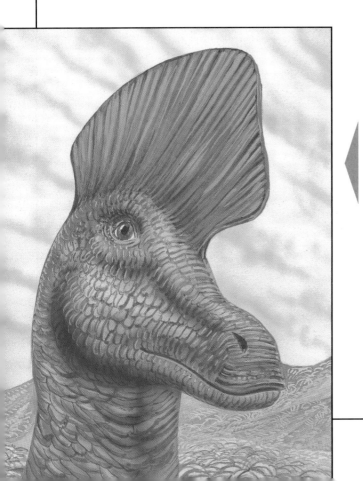

Lambeosaurus

Crested, plant-eating **Lambeosaurus** was 49 feet (15 m) long, a Late Cretaceous hadrosaur found in North America and Mexico. It was named after the famous American dinosaurologist Lawrence Lambe, who lived from 1863 to 1919.

GALLERY-2

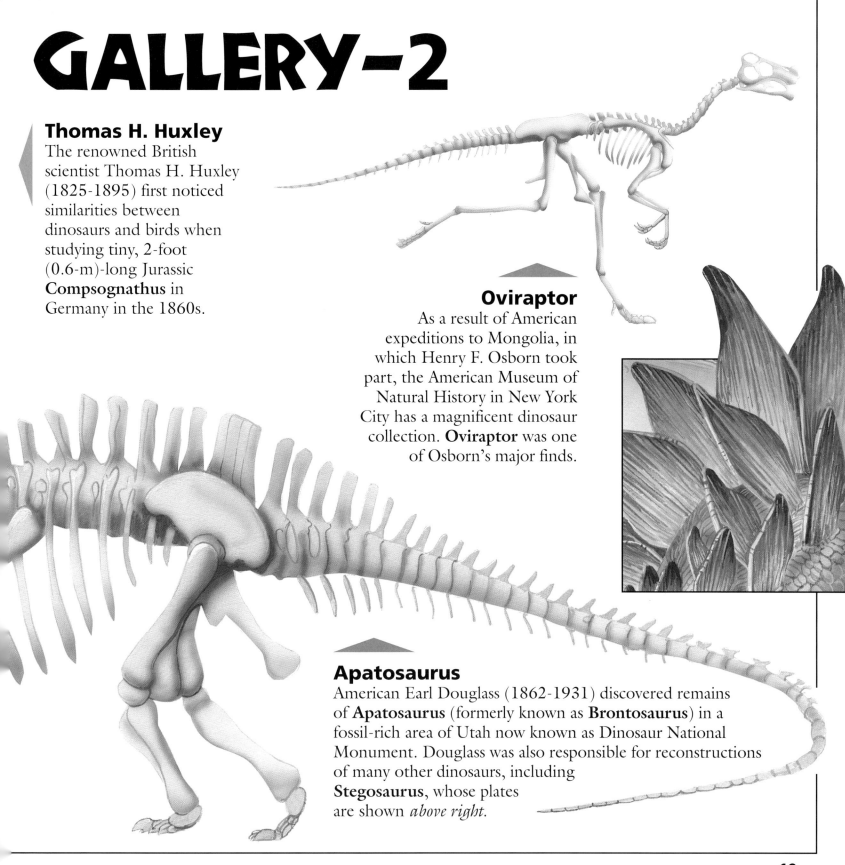

Thomas H. Huxley

The renowned British scientist Thomas H. Huxley (1825-1895) first noticed similarities between dinosaurs and birds when studying tiny, 2-foot (0.6-m)-long Jurassic **Compsognathus** in Germany in the 1860s.

Oviraptor

As a result of American expeditions to Mongolia, in which Henry F. Osborn took part, the American Museum of Natural History in New York City has a magnificent dinosaur collection. **Oviraptor** was one of Osborn's major finds.

Apatosaurus

American Earl Douglass (1862-1931) discovered remains of **Apatosaurus** (formerly known as **Brontosaurus**) in a fossil-rich area of Utah now known as Dinosaur National Monument. Douglass was also responsible for reconstructions of many other dinosaurs, including **Stegosaurus**, whose plates are shown *above right*.

DISCOVERY

Spinosaurus

German paleontologist Ernst Stromer von Reichenbach gave the name *Spinosaurus* to the 50-foot (15-m)-long Cretaceous dinosaur he found in Africa. This predatory giant had an unusual sail running all the way down its back.

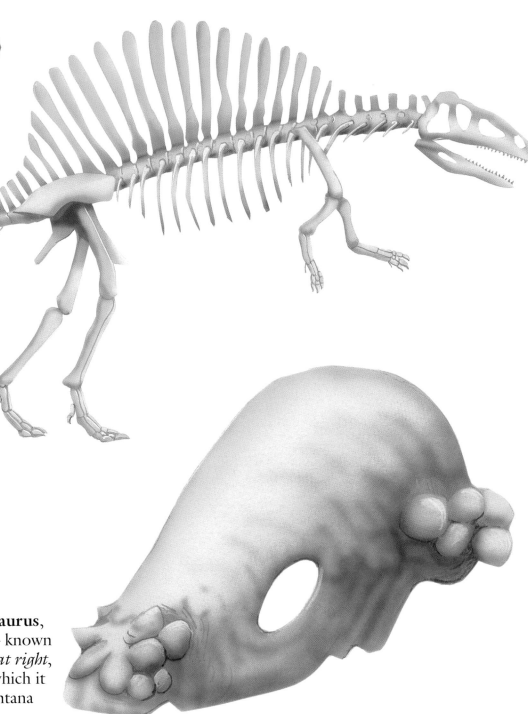

Pachycephalosaurus

The extraordinary **Pachycephalosaurus**, which was 15 feet (4.5 m) long — known for its tough, domed skull, *shown at right*, and the head-to-head combat in which it engaged — was discovered in Montana in 1940 by William Winkley.

GALLERY-3

Luis Alvarez
Together with his father, Walter Alvarez, this American scientist put forth the view that extinction of the dinosaurs occurred 65 million years ago as the result of a giant asteroid hitting our planet.

Ouranosaurus
The name *Ouranosaurus,* meaning "brave monitor lizard," was given to this plant-eating, sail-backed, Cretaceous dinosaur, which was 23 feet (7 m) long, by the French paleontologist Philippe Taquet in 1976.

Footprints
The discovery of fossilized footprints has enabled paleontologists to confirm what sort of feet different types of dinosaurs had. Scientists determined how fast they could move by measuring the distance between the tracks.

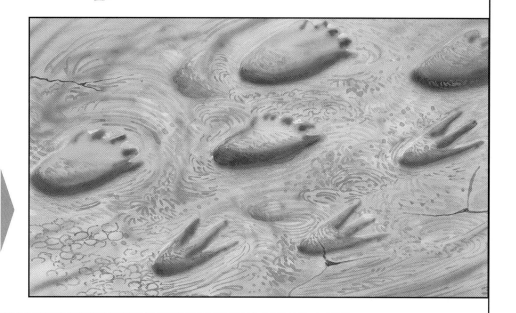

MAJOR CHINESE FINDS

Dinosaur bones and teeth have been discovered in many parts of the huge expanse of territory that now comprises mainland China.

For about 170 million years, the skeleton of a magnificent Jurassic carnivore lay buried deep in Dashanpu Quarry, in Sichuan Province of Central China, before it was discovered. No one knows how this dinosaur, which became **Gasosaurus**, died; it may have been natural causes or the result of some cataclysmic event. It is also possible that it was overcome by an even larger predator.

We can assume that for a long while after the creature's flesh had decomposed, the skull and vertebrae of this theropod looked very much like they do in the reconstruction shown *above* — before becoming fossilized and broken up by the ravages of time.

Gasosaurus was named by the esteemed Chinese dinosaurologist Zhiming Dong in honor of the gas industry that had contributed considerable funds toward its excavation. At 13 feet (4 m) in length, it was only about one-third the size of gigantic **Tyrannosaurus rex**. However, it had strongly clawed hands and sharp, daggerlike teeth with serrated edges, like those of a modern steak knife, as you can see within its deep, strong jaws.

More dinosaur remains have been found in China and North America than anywhere else in the

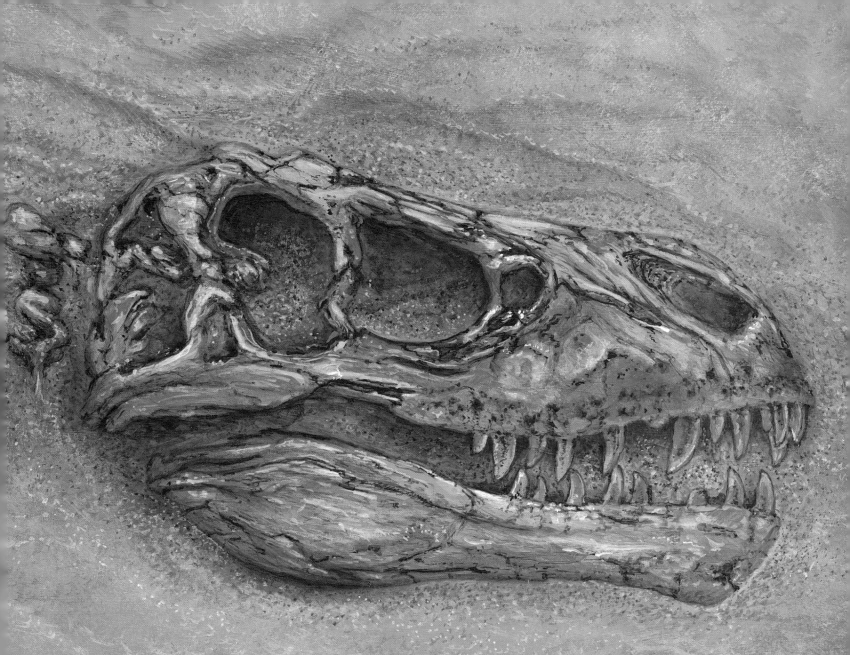

world. Some of the discoveries in these regions are of dinosaurs that must have migrated long distances, or that also lived in different parts of the world. Others, though, as far as scientists can tell from discoveries made so far, seem to have been exclusive to what is now China.

Tuojiangosaurus was 23 feet (7 m) long and one of the dinosaurs unique to China. It was named by Yihong Zhang and his colleagues, the paleontologists who first found the stegosaurid from Jurassic times.

Mamenchisaurus, also found in China, was named by Chung Chien Young. It was a giant sauropod with an extraordinarily long neck and more vertebrae than any other known creature. **Microceratops**, a tiny plant-eater only 30 inches (76 cm) long with a small neck frill, was found by the Swedish paleontologist Anders Bohlin. It also seems to have lived exclusively in China.

Many renowned Chinese paleontologists, together with experts from around the world, continue to make discoveries, unearthing both skeletons and eggs of various dinosaurs. Who knows what future digs may yield from Chinese soil!

FAMOUS MISTAKES

Even the experts sometimes make an error when reconstructing the skeleton of a dinosaur from its remains, occasionally with amusing results.

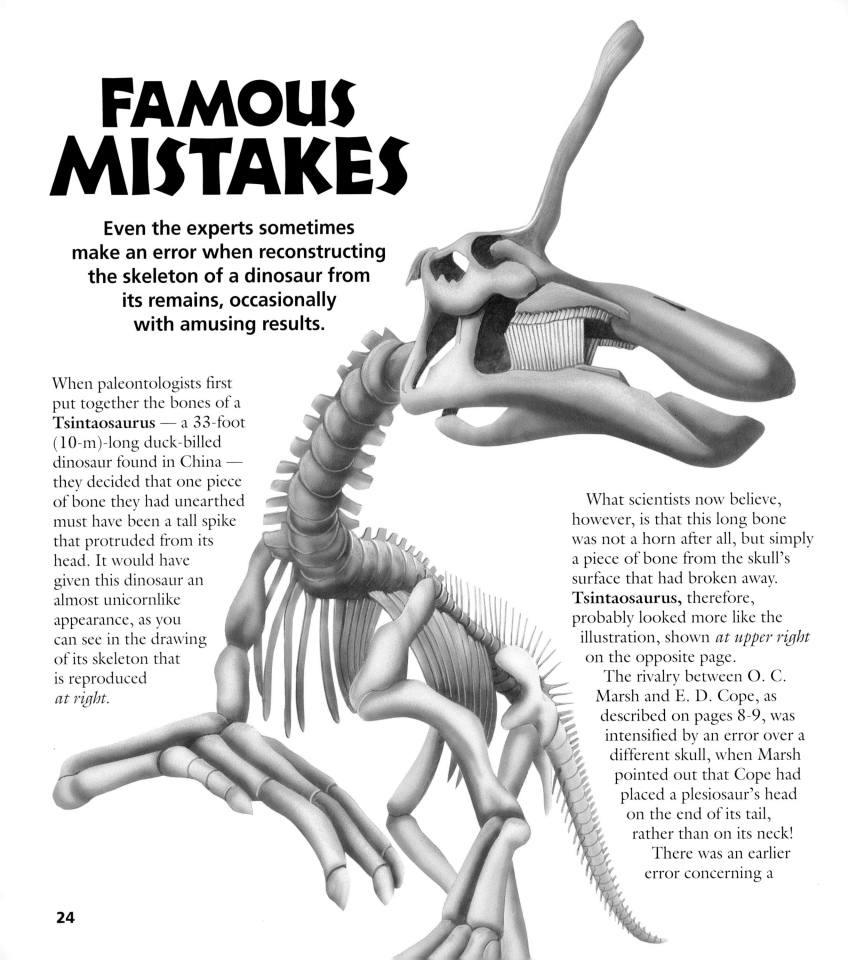

When paleontologists first put together the bones of a **Tsintaosaurus** — a 33-foot (10-m)-long duck-billed dinosaur found in China — they decided that one piece of bone they had unearthed must have been a tall spike that protruded from its head. It would have given this dinosaur an almost unicornlike appearance, as you can see in the drawing of its skeleton that is reproduced *at right*.

What scientists now believe, however, is that this long bone was not a horn after all, but simply a piece of bone from the skull's surface that had broken away. **Tsintaosaurus,** therefore, probably looked more like the illustration, shown *at upper right* on the opposite page.

The rivalry between O. C. Marsh and E. D. Cope, as described on pages 8-9, was intensified by an error over a different skull, when Marsh pointed out that Cope had placed a plesiosaur's head on the end of its tail, rather than on its neck! There was an earlier error concerning a dinosaur find that occurred even before dinosaurs had been identified and named as a group. The mistake was made by a seventeenth-century professor at Oxford University named Robert Plot. He had been presented with what scientists now think must have been the thighbone of a **Megalosaurus**, which grew to 30 feet (9 m) in length and stood more than twice the height of today's average man. Though the fossil itself has long been lost, excellent drawings of it, dating from 1677 when Plot first tried to identify the fossil, still exist.

Plot's opinion was that it might be the thighbone of an elephant, brought to England by the Romans, though he admitted there were no written records of these creatures ever having been brought to the British Isles. He even wondered if it might have been a bone from some member of a giant race of humans that had once existed.

Thumbs up

Another major mistake was made when the highly respected anatomist Sir Richard Owen helped architect Benjamin Waterhouse Hawkins reconstruct an **Iguanodon** skeleton. Owen thought this dinosaur must have looked like a rhinoceros, and so assumed that it had a horn. A bone was therefore placed on the **Iguanodon**'s skull. Of course, it was soon discovered that this fossil was actually **Iguanodon**'s famous spiked thumb!

End of the matter?

There have been many unusual theories, too, about what led to the extinction of the dinosaurs. One Russian scientist speculated that dinosaurs died out because of rickets, first becoming calcium deficient and then perishing as a result.

The most widely accepted theory is that our planet was hit by an asteroid at the end of the Cretaceous era, blocking sunlight so that plants could not flourish. Herbivores starved, and so, in turn, did the carnivores.

ECCENTRIC'S ERROR

The Hungarian dinosaurologist Baron Nopsca made a dramatic error in 1929 when he announced that all crested hadrosaurs must have been males, and that female hadrosaurs had no crests at all. However, crested hadrosaurs have been found in different strata of the Earth, indicating that they must have lived thousands of years apart from the females. This would make mating, and therefore survival, unlikely, to say the least, if his theory was true! Baron Nopsca was somewhat eccentric and extremist in his views, with an ultimate aim to declare himself King of Albania.

CRACKING FINDS

Discovery of dinosaur eggs confirmed that these prehistoric creatures did not give birth to live young, and therefore were probably not mammals.

Roy Chapman Andrews and his team were absolutely astounded. There, in the rock, were the remains of a whole clutch of fossilized eggs — dinosaur eggs! Even more exciting, there seemed to be several nests in the area, all containing elongated eggs that had been laid in neatly arranged circular formations.

The expedition, organized by the American Museum of Natural History in New York, had set off for Mongolia in 1922 in search of early human remains, since Andrews was convinced that *homo sapiens* must have evolved first in Asia.

A caravan of camels was used to transport the expedition's equipment, while the scientists and team members traveled in the comparative luxury of a fleet of motor vehicles. Following a long and arduous journey, the dig was begun, but no human remains were unearthed. The dinosaur eggs that they found during their quest, however, more than made up for their initial disappointment — even though this discovery was entirely unexpected.

Some experts believe that dinosaur eggs may have come to light many thousands of years before Andrews' discovery. They have suggested that fragments of shells might have been used for decorative jewelry by primitive peoples. Several dinosaur eggs had been unearthed and identified in France a few years prior to Andrews' expedition. His excavation's finds, however — at an area known colloquially as Flaming Cliffs because of the local red sandstone — were the first to include entire nests. The eggs inside them were described as resembling large baked potatoes!

Andrews' team found other remarkable remains, too, when they made further expeditions to the Gobi Desert. Among their discoveries was **Oviraptor**, the beaked, birdlike dinosaur given a name meaning "egg-thief" because its remains were found over a nest. Today, it is believed to have died there while protecting its own eggs from a nest-robber.

Velociraptor, a bipedal predator with a large switchblade claw on the second toe of each foot, was unearthed there, too; there is even a skeleton that shows it in battle with a **Protoceratops**. Armored **Pinacosaurus** was 18 feet (5.5 m) long and a plant-eater with a clubbed tail; it was also from this region. Mongolia's Gobi Desert was a huge dinosaur graveyard, and it continues to yield superb specimens today.

Inside information

Over the years, many other egg finds have been made in places as far apart as Uruguay, Romania, India, and North America. An especially exciting discovery was made in 1995 by another team of American paleontologists. They unearthed an egg of the Cretaceous herbivore **Saltasaurus** from Argentina. The egg was in excellent condition, and a scan of its insides revealed the remains of a fossilized embryo in a very early stage of development. Evidence of a baby **Oviraptor** has also been found within the partly worn-away shell of a fossilized egg. A number of eminent paleontologists, including Roy Chapman Andrews earlier this century, have made what could suitably be described as "cracking" finds!

NESTING SITES

The 90-million-year-old eggs shown *at right* were laid by a **Protoceratops.** They were part of a large nesting site found in Mongolia's Gobi Desert. The eggs were oval, as you can see, and found near the skeletal remains of mature ceratopsians. Other nearby nests had round eggs; these probably would have hatched into another type of dinosaur. In 1978, paleontologists Bob Makela and Jack Horner made an equally outstanding discovery of a **Maiasaura** nesting site in Montana. Their finds were so extensive and important that the area was dubbed Egg Mountain.

RECENT GIANT FINDS

Over the last few years, skeletal remains of several dinosaurs of fantastic proportions have been unearthed in places as far apart as North Africa and South America.

Giganotosaurus's teeth were like scimitars, ideal for slicing at flesh. The meat-eater's sudden appearance meant that the herd of herbivores, each about the size of a human today, stood no chance of survival. The gigantic beast could simply snap them up one by one and then gulp down large chunks of flesh or possibly swallow the prey whole. At times, it would attack much larger plant-eaters, as heavy or perhaps even heavier than itself, by biting into them. The unfortunate victim would be left to bleed to death while the feasting began.

Over 40 feet (12 m) long and weighing some 8 tons, Cretaceous

Giganotosaurus was first discovered in an area known as Patagonia in Argentina, South America, in 1993. It is the largest predator found to date in this part of the world and is estimated to have been even larger than **Tyrannosaurus rex**.

Another discovery two years later — this time, in Morocco, North Africa — led paleontologist Paul Sereno from the University of Chicago to a noteworthy

conclusion. This newly unearthed dinosaur, **Carcharodontosaurus** (with a name meaning "shark-toothed reptile"), seems to have had a remarkable similarity to **Giganotosaurus**. Experts believe

it is possible that the two species were closely related. South America and Africa had remained joined for many millions of years in prehistoric times, even after giant landmasses started to break up.

Sometimes only a few bones of what was a massive dinosaur are discovered, making the work of the paleontologist more difficult. **Argentinosaurus**, for instance, also from Patagonia, is only known from part of its body. Nevertheless, experts can tell that this massive sauropod weighed as much as 100 tons. If they ever find a complete skeleton, it will require years of work to unearth its remains!

GLOSSARY

anatomy — the arrangement and relationship of the parts of a living thing.

asteroid — one of the thousands of small planets that orbit the Sun between Mars and Jupiter.

bipedal — related to an animal that has two legs.

browse — to feed on the tender shoots, twigs, and leaves of trees and shrubs.

carnivore — a meat-eater.

ceratopsian — a type of dinosaur with horns, such as Triceratops.

clutch (n) — a nest of eggs; a brood, or group, of animals recently hatched from eggs.

Cretaceous times — the final era of the dinosaurs, lasting from 144-65 million years ago.

curator — a person in charge of a museum collection or exhibit.

dinosaurologists — scientists who study dinosaurs.

embryo — an animal in the first stage of development before birth.

eminent — standing out above all others; extraordinary.

excavated — dug out; exposed by digging.

foliage — the leaves of a tree, shrub, or plant.

fossilized — embedded and preserved in rocks, resin, or other material.

hadrosaur — a member of a group of duck-billed dinosaurs.

herbivore — a plant-eater.

ichthyosaur — an extinct marine reptile that had a fishlike body and long snout.

Jurassic times — the middle era of the dinosaurs, lasting from 213-144 million years ago.

massive — heavy and bulky; weighty.

mimic — to copy or imitate someone or something.

oblique — slanting or sloping; not straightforward.

omnivore — an animal that eats both plants and meat.

paleontologist — a scientist who studies geologic periods of the past as they are known from fossil remains.

plesiosaur — a long-necked, prehistoric marine reptile.

prosauropod — moderately long-necked dinosaurs, all herbivores, principally from Triassic times.

prospector — someone who looks for valuable minerals, such as gold.

pterosaur — a member of a group of extinct flying reptiles.

reconstruction — the reassembling of something, such as the skeleton of a dinosaur.

renowned — honored; famous.

rickets — a disease that is caused by a deficiency of vitamin D, which results in soft and deformed bones.

rivals — one of two or more trying to get the same thing; competitors.

sauropod — a member of a group of long-necked plant-eating dinosaurs, primarily from Jurassic times.

scimitars — curved sabers, or weapons, with very sharp blades.

theropod — a member of a group of meat-eating bipedal dinosaurs.

Triassic times — the first era of the dinosaurs, lasting from 249-213 million years ago.

unearthed — dug out of the ground; discovered.

vertebra — one of the small bones that form an animal's backbone, or spine.

MORE BOOKS TO READ

Dating Dinosaurs and Other Old Things.
  Karen Liptak (Millbrook Press)

Dinosaurs: Unearthing the Secrets of Ancient Beasts.
  Don Nardo (Lucent Books)

Discover Dinosaurs: Become a Dinosaur Detective.
  Christopher McGowan (Addison Wesley)

Graveyards of the Dinosaurs: What It's Like to
  Discover Prehistoric Creatures. Shelley Tanaka
  (Hyperion Books for Children)

Hunting the Dinosaur and Other Prehistoric Animals.
  Dougal Dixon (Gareth Stevens)

Jack Horner: Living With Dinosaurs. Don Lessem
  (Scientific American Books for Young Readers)

Let's Go Dinosaur Tracking. Miriam Schlein
  (HarperCollins)

Looking at New Dinosaur Discoveries. Tamara Green
  (Gareth Stevens)

The New Dinosaur Collection (series). (Gareth Stevens)

Tracking Dinosaurs in the Gobi. Margery Facklam
  (Twenty-First Century Books)

World of Dinosaurs (series). (Gareth Stevens)

VIDEOS

Did Comets Kill The Dinosaurs? (Gareth Stevens)

Digging Dinosaurs. (PBS Video)

Digging Up Dinosaurs. (Great Plains National
  Instructional Television Library)

Dinosaurs. (Smithsonian Video)

Dinosaurs: Remains to Be Seen. (Public Media, Inc.)

Flesh on the Bones. (PBS Video)

I Dig Fossils. (Mazon Productions)

Learning About Dinosaurs. (Trans-Atlantic Video)

WEB SITES

www.clpgh.org/cmnh/discovery/

www.dinodon.com/index.html

www.dinofest.org/

www.dinosauria.com/

www.mwc.mus.co.us/dinosaurs/

www.ZoomDinosaurs.com

Due to the dynamic nature of the Internet, some web sites stay current longer than others. To find additional web sites, use a reliable search engine with one or more of the following keywords to help you locate more information about dinosaurs. Keywords: *Mary Anning, carnivores, fossils, paleontology, prehistoric.*

INDEX